Steve's Dreams

Steve and the Sabretooth Tiger

First published in 2014
by Firefly Press
25 Gabalfa Road, Llandaff North, Cardiff, CF14 2JJ
www.fireflypress.co.uk

Text © Dan Anthony 2014
Illustrations © Huw Aaron 2014

A CIP catalogue record of this book is available from the British Library.

Print ISBN: 978-1-910080-06-1
Epub ISBN: 978-1-910080-07-8

This book has been published with the support of the
Welsh Books Council.

Typeset by: Elaine Sharples

Printed and bound by: Bell and Bain, Glasgow

Steve's Dreams

Steve and the Sabretooth Tiger

by
Dan Anthony
illustrated by Huw Aaron

Firefly

Something Lurks

Life is really dangerous. They don't tell you in school and they try not to mention it at home. It's like a secret grown-ups think children can't cope with. Everyone tells me I worry too much, but I think maybe they're the ones who are pretending. Life is too scary for grown-ups.

I remember the package arriving. It was made of brown cardboard, half envelope, half box – the sort of thing they use when you buy stuff online. But this was from the library. I know that because on the outside, in big black letters, it said: FROM THE LIBRARY. I know it was for me because then it said: FOR STEVE. When Mum showed it to me she raised

one eyebrow, as if I owed them money or I'd lost one of their books or something.

I didn't open it. I knew I hadn't ordered any books. It was a trick. I've got a nose for trouble, and that parcel was full of it. I left it on the kitchen table and nobody said any more about it.

It stayed there for a long time. Sometimes it got covered with other things: magazines, packets of cereal, bottles of nail varnish, sugar, salt and pepper.

But every now and again it would make its way to the top of the pile, as if to say, '*Look at me.*'

'*Open me.*'

I live in a town called Pendown just outside a big city. My part is the Oliphant Circles Estate. Oliphant Circles is a long, round road that twists in on itself – like the swirl on a snail's shell. People from Pendown and Oliphant Circles stay in Oliphant Circles and Pendown. They go round and round.

In school the teachers are always telling us how good it is to live in a 'new town'. But it doesn't look very new. It's a lot older than me and I'm already nine. My mum was born in Pendown and she's definitely not new. Newport, the city we're closest to, doesn't have ships and it isn't new either. Nothing is what it says.

Don't get me wrong. I like it here. We've got supermarkets, McDonalds, a motorway and a multiplex cinema. There's even a small railway

station. I keep my eyes open around Oliphant Circles. I want to help people. They don't realise that wherever you go around here, something lurks.

On the morning of 29th July I opened my eyes quickly, like I always do, and checked for danger. I looked up through the skylight over my bunk. I scanned the sky for unusual signs: missile trails, asteroid flashes, the telltale zap lines of alien war beams. I always do this. Usually the coast is clear.

Today all I could make out was a few seagulls floating in the blue sky like tiny faraway kites. It was going to be a hot day. Most people think sunny days are great. But too much solar radiation is bad news. My advice is simple – if it's a nice day, don't go out without an umbrella.

I have the top bunk. My brother Kyled sleeps on the one below. He's five. He's not allowed up here because he keeps jumping off. I'm responsible. I know that if I have a bad nightmare, I could jump up, fall off the bed and crash to the floor. So I sleep on the wall side.

I like to lie up here and watch the stars, or the clouds, or the trees on the hills that surround my town. If anybody has a go at Pendown, I'll be the first to know.

2

29th July

In the holidays, things are pretty chilled in my house. My sisters, Miffany and Jaydee, don't usually get up in the mornings. They're fifteen. They're twins. They can do whatever they want.

It was ten past nine when I walked into the kitchen to get my cereal and feed Groucho. Everybody was there: Jaydee, Miffany, Kyled, Mum and, on Skype, Dad.

'Sorry,' said Dad, 'I'm losing the connec...'

I saw his face on the screen. Then the screen flickered and the connection went. Everybody turned on me.

'Steve!' chorused my sisters. 'You lost Dad.'

'I never did anything,' I said. 'I didn't know we had him in the first place.'

'I thought you were asleep,' said Mum.

'I'm never asleep,' I said. 'Somebody's got to be on the lookout.' I pointed at my sisters. 'They're the ones who sleep all the time.'

Jaydee yawned. She was dressed in a Dalmatian onesie and she had long, straight blonde hair; Miffany was a tiger with curly red hair. They're very un-identical twins.

'Did you spot any incoming missiles, Steve?' asked Jaydee, ruffling my hair.

'I think we're OK for today,' I said.

'Intruders? Burglars? Spies?' asked Miffany. She always liked listening to what I'd found.

'I thought we'd been captured by kidnappers in the night,' I said, 'but it turned out to be a dream.'

Miff bent down and whispered in my ear. She had

a message from Dad. She said she'd told him I was doing my checks. He said that he was glad there was someone around who could see the bigger picture. He told her to tell me not to worry for being late.

Jaydee moved towards the kitchen door.

'Come on, Miff, we're outta here.'

They took their bowls of cereal and slid out of the kitchen back up to their room to watch TV.

'Do you remember what day it is?' said Mum quietly as I started putting food in Groucho's bowl.

'It's 29th July,' I said gloomily. I'd been thinking about it for ages. At four thirty I had my Appointment.

'Then why didn't you come

down earlier?' she asked, cupping her 'Best Mum in the World' mug with both hands. 'For Dad's birthday?'

I stopped filling the bowl. I knew there was another reason why 29th July was important.

My dad works in the oil industry. He's hardly ever at home. He goes to Mexico, Scotland, Uzbekistan, Kyrgystan, Kazakhstan. He says, 'if it's got a "Stan" in it, that's where I am.' His name is Stan, by the way.

'Sorry,' I said.

After feeding Groucho I took some toast and sat down at the table. I looked at the package, the one from the library. It was on its way back to the top of the pile again.

Mum sipped her coffee and put some more cereal in Kyled's bowl. He scowled at me. Jaydee and Miffany are great, they share things with me, they don't mind me borrowing their computers or watching their TV and they always like to know what level of alert we're on. But Kyled's not like that. He doesn't share.

'Mum,' said Kyled, 'did Dad run away when he saw Steve?'

'Of course not,' said Mum as she filled Kyled's bowl right to the top. 'He's such a big bonny boy,' she said. 'Eat up, Kyled.'

Kyled glared at me as he spooned the new bowlful into his mouth. His bright blue eyes caught the sunlight flashing in through the kitchen windows. I'd been monitoring Kyled's rapid growth rate over the past two years. He was already the biggest boy in the infant school and he was strong too. He was becoming a monster-boy.

'Steve kept me awake last night,' said Kyled.

Mum sipped her tea.

'He kept tossing and turning and screaming out loud,' said Kyled.

'Shut up, Kyled,' I said.

'Nooo, Aaaargh. Nooooo. Aaaargh. All night long,' said Kyled.

'Is this right?' asked Mum. She rested the palm of her hand on my forehead. I felt foolish.

'He's talking rubbish,' I said, 'just like he always does. He's a rubbish-talker, that Kyled.'

Kyled licked his bowl, just like Groucho, who, in case you are wondering, is our dog. A small, brown Yorkshire terrier.

'Screamed all night like a little baby,' shouted Kyled, jumping down from his chair at the kitchen table. 'Waaa, waaa, waaa.'

'Kyled, why don't you go out into the garden and play on the trampoline,' said Mum. 'I'll count the bounces.'

'Nice one,' said Kyled and he rushed out into the garden.

I kept an eye on Mum as she watched Kyled. She started to count, 'One, two, three…'

'I wasn't trying to keep Kyled awake,' I said, reassuringly. 'It was just a dream.'

'Why don't you go outside and enjoy yourself too, Steve? It's a lovely morning,' she said. 'And try not to worry so much. Most things turn out all right in the end.'

'Outside?' I looked through the kitchen window at the blue sky above Kyled's bouncing head. 'Can I borrow your umbrella?'

Mum ignored me. She must have lost her brolly.

'… eleven, twelve, thirteen…'

As she counted the bounces, Mum picked a magazine off the pile of stuff at the end of the table.

I saw it again. Those big black letters: 'FROM THE LIBRARY. FOR STEVE.' The parcel had come back to the surface.

I reached out and touched it. Perhaps today was the day I would open it.

Mum stood by the kitchen window half watching Kyled bounce as she flicked through the pages of the magazine.

'… thirty-three, thirty-four, thirty-five…'

I turned the package over in my hands. It felt

explosive. Perhaps if I opened it there would be an almighty Kerbooom!! Goodbye Steve. Hello invasion force sweeping through Oliphant Circles. That was a strong possibility. But there were other people who wanted me out of the picture. Spies don't like me because I'm always trying to spot them. Alien invaders have to keep clear of my patch of sky because I'm always checking for them.

'... forty-seven, forty-eight, forty-nine...'

On the other hand – maybe the package was from someone who needed help.

'Why don't you go and play football?' asked Mum as she

counted and read the magazine. Mum always says she's very good at multi-tasking.

'Go out and play, Steve. Please,' she added, 'we've got to go at twelve.'

Twelve?! I thought that my Appointment was at four thirty. Suddenly my time had been cut by half. That was when I realised I had nothing to lose. If I wanted to find out what was in the package, I needed to look right now.

I ripped the cardboard.

Mum turned and watched. She stopped counting.

'It's about time you opened that,' she said, 'I checked at the library. We haven't ordered anything.'

'As if this was sent by a real librarian,' I muttered as I stuck my hand in. I felt something soft. I closed my eyes tight and pulled it out.

Nothing exploded.

I opened my eyes.

It was a hat. A green baseball hat with 'Library' written on it in big yellow letters. I put it on. It fitted perfectly. It had a big peak to keep the sun off and was made of good material. It was just right for keeping the solar radiation off, better than an umbrella.

I smiled. Now it was OK to go out the back to play football.

'Somebody likes you,' joked Mum, 'at the library.'

3

The Sarsaparilla Kid

The back garden of our house isn't exactly great to play in. There's a patio between the kitchen and the side path. I'm not allowed to play there because Mum's got her terracotta pots all over the place. Then there's the lawn, which is really a patch of earth with tufts of straggly grass on it, Groucho wees on it and Kyled keeps his trampoline there.

It's more like a house than a trampoline. It's got an entrance, which you unzip, and walls made out of netting so that Kyled doesn't fly off into someone else's garden. He spends hours in there, throwing himself around like a Tasmanian devil. And he makes weird noises. He yells and shouts. It can be disturbing if you don't know he's actually having a good time.

I picked up my football and went into the garden, and then through the gate into the back lane.

It was hot in the back lane, hotter than usual: too hot to kick the ball off the wall for long. In the end I sat on the ball and threw little sticks for Groucho to fetch. But Groucho was hot too. His tongue hung out of his mouth and he kept looking at me with his big black eyes as if to say: 'You know I normally like fetching sticks? Well, today I'm not so sure. It's boiling.'

'Hi,' said a familiar voice.

Toby, or 'Tobes' as he likes to be known, had shown up.

I looked up at Toby. He was wearing the Villa Real t-shirt my mum had given him after we came back from Spain. He was bigger than me, older than me, and, although I feel bad for saying this, sometimes a bit dull. Even throwing little sticks for Groucho was more fun than Tobes.

'Hi,' he said again, 'hot, isn't it?'

'Yes,' I said.

'Cool library hat.'

I nodded. Library hats aren't cool, I know that for a fact. If Toby thinks something is cool you can pretty much guarantee it isn't.

'Where did you get it from?'

I wanted to say, 'The library, *duh*.' But that wasn't true. The truth was, I didn't know where it had come from – all I knew is that it was an excellent anti-solar flare radiation device, brilliant if you don't have an umbrella.

'Around,' I said.

'What you doing?' asked Toby.

'Enjoying myself,' I said. 'My mum asked me to go outside and enjoy myself.' I didn't say it was because she knows this was probably my last day on earth. Because of my Appointment.

'You going down the shop?' asked Toby.

I looked up at him. He was thirteen. Surely he was smart enough to realise that sitting on a football

throwing sticks for the dog because you've been told

to enjoy yourself is not the same as going down the

shop. What he meant was that he was going down

the shop and he wanted me to go too.

'I'm going down the shop,' he announced.

I found myself walking with Toby, kicking the ball along. Groucho trotted behind us. I explained to Toby about the sunspots and global warming. Looking back, I suppose you could say I was enjoying myself.

'No way, Steve,' said Toby, wide-eyed after I'd told him how hot things were going to get. 'Better get a drink then, to cool us down. They've got sarsaparilla. D'you want a sarsaparilla?'

Toby had this thing about drinks – he said it was good to buy the weird ones because if you didn't, the shop wouldn't bother getting them anymore.

'Is it safe?' I asked.

'I've been drinking it for ages and it hasn't done me any harm,' said Toby. 'It's a cool brew.'

I nodded. No doubt sarsaparilla was very uncool.

When Mum came into the back lane at ten past twelve, I was showing Toby how to download a temperature-recording app onto his phone and Groucho was lapping sarsaparilla from an old curry carton.

'Sorry, Toby,' I said, when I saw Mum, 'this is it.'

Toby didn't understand.

I shook his hand and told him there was a good chance this would be our last meeting.

At 4.30 pm I was due to be strapped into a chair. Just imagine. It's the end of a very hot day. The dentist has been seeing patients for hours. I sit in her chair, the plastic all sticky and sweaty. She holds up one of those prongy things for poking around your teeth. I close my eyes. Then she comes towards me and – trips on a cable. She pushes her hands out to stop herself falling into me. She forgets about the prongy thing. Pow!

No more Steve.

In this heat, last thing on a Friday, it was bound to happen.

'Goodbye, Toby,' I said, 'remember what I told you.'

Toby had already forgotten.

4

Two People Survive

Mum's a teacher, so during the summer holidays she's quite free, although she runs extra classes for adult learners. She uses the money from those lessons to pay for things like Kyled's trampoline and her terracotta pots.

Mum is head of Spanish at Pendown Comprehensive School. There is only one Spanish teacher in the school – Mum. She's what they call a one woman band. Spain to Mum is hot and lovely but far away. Whereas Wales is wet, miserable and right by here. She lives in Oliphant Circles, but she thinks she's in Spain. I keep telling her, 'Mum, you're not Spanish.' Mum says one day we'll all move to Spain.

This was the plan: I would sit at the back of Mum's Spanish lesson. She'd give me some really manky old crayons and some bits of paper so that I could do drawing. She wouldn't give me an iPad or laptop or any of the things her students had, because she said I might break it. Basically, I'd be expected to be invisible for two hours. Then she'd take me to the dentist. Then we'd go to the supermarket.

As we drove along the Western Distributor Road I tried to persuade her to leave out the dentist part.

'Mrs Etherington is a brilliant dentist,' said Mum.

'She never has accidents. All she wants to do is give you a check-up.'

'In this heat,' I said, 'even the best people lose their concentration.'

'Please be quiet in the lesson, Steve,' said Mum, as she pulled off the dual carriageway and drove towards the old church where they hold the Spanish class. 'Could you take that hat off?'

I pulled the library hat tighter down over my head. It made me feel safe.

Mum stopped the car with a judder outside the big arched doorway to St Esther's Church.

The desks were arranged in a big square in the middle of the church hall and the students sat around the square. I say students, they were actually just old people. Some of them had houses in Spain, one of them, one of the worst at speaking Spanish, actually had a yacht which he kept near Barcelona.

So there I was, sitting at an old desk in the old church hall. The sunlight streamed through the high windows. I held a big fat crayon and some scrappy bits of paper left over from Sunday School. I was writing the story of

29th July, so that Jay, Miff and Kyled would know what happened to their brother on this dreadful day. As Mum asked the old people what they'd bought in the pretend Spanish supermarket, I put down my last words and drew a picture of the prongy thing. I had about two hours to live. Then it was Death by Dentist.

I was trying to think what else to put when something happened. Mum asked a lady in a blue dress with big golden flowers on it whether she preferred black or green olives. This lady, Mrs Prothero, couldn't understand the question, but she didn't want the other students to know, because she considered herself to be one of the smart ones. Before she retired, Mrs Prothero was the Librarian at Oliphant Circles' Library and she couldn't stand getting things wrong.

'*Espera uno momentito,*' said Mrs Prothero carefully.

I looked across from my corner. All the students were looking at Mrs Prothero. My mum looked at her. My mum can be quite scary when she's being a teacher.

Mum asked Mrs Prothero again, '*Aceitunas negras o verdes?*'

Mrs Prothero knew she'd been asked a question, she was pretending that she knew the answer. She looked one way, then shrugged, then another and shrugged again.

Mum tapped her fingers.

Mr Rochdale coughed and whispered at the same time. 'Olives,' he spluttered.

'I know, I know,' said Mrs Prothero, '*olivas*. Hmmmm.'

Mum looked at Mrs Prothero.

We all looked at Mrs Prothero.

Did she prefer black or green olives?

It was the most important question in the world.

I put my crayon down. I pushed the brim of my hat back on my forehead.

I could see beads of sweat on Mrs Prothero's face.

She was going to have to fess up. She didn't understand the question.

She looked around desperately. And then her eyes locked on me.

'Black or green?' I muttered.

But then Mrs Prothero started coughing and spluttering. She rolled off her chair onto the floor and started writhing around on the dusty old wood. Her grey hair spilled out of her tight little bun.

'Water...' she cried.

For a moment Mum and the Spanish class didn't move. They were all thinking that Mrs Prothero was just pretending to choke, to avoid the question.

Mum walked around to her. She knelt down.

'Come on,' she said, 'I'll get you a glass of water. I asked if you prefer black or green olives.'

But Mrs Prothero got worse. Her eyes fixed on me and then, as if possessed by some strange spirit, she began crawling towards me.

'The boy,' she hissed. 'The library,' she snarled.

Her hand extended towards me, her index finger stretched out, pointing straight at me. The old librarian was crawling across the church hall as if she wanted to eat me.

I shrank back.

Mum tried to hold Mrs Prothero. 'Help me!' she shouted.

In an instant the Spanish students sprang to life.

Doctor Pearson, who had a villa outside Malaga, pulled back her pointing finger.

'Go to the library,' whispered Mrs Prothero at me, then she fainted.

5

The Dentist

She came round quite quickly. As Doctor Pearson loosened Mrs Prothero's orange scarf, I could hear her saying that she thought she'd be OK if she could have a sit down. They hoisted her up into a chair next to me and brought her plastic cups of water. Before long Mrs Prothero was sitting with a cup of tea and a biscuit on one side of her and her head between her knees. Doctor Pearson said that it was some kind of nervous disorder and … guess what? The heat.

'I'm terribly sorry,' she whispered to me, as the lesson continued, 'I've never felt like that before.'

I nodded. I knew Mrs Prothero's attack was brought on by global warming, sunspots and not being able to understand Spanish. I had other things to worry about.

'That was the worst class I've ever taken,' said Mum, crashing the gears so that they made the car jump and bump along the Western Distributor Road. We swung off and entered a leafy avenue. I decided to have one last go at saving myself.

'Stop the car!' I said.

Mum didn't stop the car.

'Mum, this is a mistake,' I said.

Mum said nothing.

'Mum, you've got to believe me,' I said. 'I've got something important to say!'

She stopped the car outside a big old stone house. On the wall in front of the garden was a shiny brass plaque:

MRS ETHERINGTON – DENTIST

'Do you believe in oracles?' I asked. I didn't get out of the car.

Mum looked straight ahead. 'What?' she sighed.

'Oracles, soothsayers, people who have the power to see into the future. A bit like the elves in *The Hobbit*.'

Mum shook her head and looked at her watch.

'Mrs Prothero's attack was a premonition. It means we're heading towards danger.'

'Steve, we're late,' said Mum opening the door.

I grabbed her arm. This was my last chance.

'Did you see her point?' I said.

'It was the hat,' said Mum. She thought for a moment. 'She's a retired librarian. I think she just got a bit confused.'

'She knew I'm in danger,' I said. 'She knew Mrs Etherington will trip on the cable and stick her prongy thing straight into my brain.'

'Steve,' said Mum, pulling away from me and onto the pavement, 'You've been coming here for years. It's just a check-up. For goodness' sake, stop being such a wimp.'

I stopped. My face went red. I felt my lip quiver. I felt like saying, 'I am not being a wimp.' But that would have been wimpy.

I said nothing. I knew that this was the brave thing to do. I had to deal with it myself. A dentist would kill me with a prongy thing. Like a brave king heading for the beheader, I stepped out of the car. I walked in silence through the neat little front garden of Mrs Etherington's surgery. I walked through the door in front of Mum. I went to the counter and gave my name to the receptionist and Mrs Etherington's head immediately popped into view from behind a white door. She looked strangely smiley.

'Steve! I've been waiting for you,' she laughed. She was practically cackling. 'You're my last patient. Once I've got you out of the way I can go and play tennis.'

I walked, stiffly, calmly. I thought about Groucho lapping up the sarsaparilla from a curry carton in the back lane. I remembered how he looked up at me, wagging his tail. I could see his sparkly black eyes. He was trying to say: 'Thanks, Steve, this stuff, whatever they call it, is great.'

Mrs Etherington waved at Mum. She asked Mum if she'd like to go to tennis too. Mum said she didn't have time.

I clambered into the big chair. I noticed that there was no helper, just as Mrs Etherington bounded over. She tripped on the cable connecting the big light to the socket.

I flinched.

'Ooops,' she laughed. 'It's just me and you today. I let Nurse Pedwell go early. It's such a nice day and he wanted to get outside.'

Mum sat on a chair. I tried to catch her eye but she avoided my glance.

The nurse was absent. Just as I had imagined. Now all Mrs Etherington had to do was get Mum out of the room and the stage would be set for the fatal accident.

'Open wide,' said Mrs Etherington. 'My, what a lovely set of gnashers you've got. That's a lovely hat you're wearing. A lot of my patients keep their hats on. It helps them relax.'

She started tapping on my teeth. 'Left upper,' she muttered, 'left upper 2,3,4.' Her face was really close to mine. I watched her blue eyes looking at my teeth. Suddenly she looked sideways, at Mum.

'I wonder if I could ask you to do me a favour?' said Mrs Etherington.

My heart was pounding. She was going to get Mum to leave the room.

'Could you ask Joyce at the reception desk to come and join us, just to check off the teeth?'

Without putting up any kind of argument, Mum walked out.

I realised, too late, that the only possible explanation was that Mum was in on it too.

My skin went cold. All I could see now was the big round silver and white light and Mrs Etherington's head. She had blondy grey hair tied back behind her ears. She approached me with the prongy thing. I closed my eyes.

When I opened my eyes, we were in the car again. Mum was driving back down the Western Distributor Road. She looked very angry. I felt weird: wobbly, fuzzy, as if I'd just been having an incredibly vivid dream. Then I remembered – I had been murdered by my dentist.

I must be a ghost.

'How could you?' I said to Mum, staring right at her.

'I beg your pardon,' she said, swerving the car into a line of traffic on the dual carriageway.

'How could you?'

'How could *you*?' she said.

'How could I what?'

'How do you feel?' she asked, with a serious look in her eye.

Then I realised I'd been brought back to the living world to help my mother and shouldn't be angry with her.

'Great,' I said, 'for a ghost.'

'Come on, Steve,' said Mum. She smiled at me. 'You worry too much, nobody's angry with you.'

Mum was clearly in shock.

'Don't be sad,' I said. 'I'm here to help. You can call me Spirit of Steve if you like.'

Mum ignored me. 'I'm afraid we haven't got time to go to the library today,' she said.

'That's all right.' I wasn't sure if ghosts went to libraries.

The next road sign we passed was new. It said:

GO TO THE LIBRARY.

I'd never seen one like that before. I don't think Mum noticed it. I didn't like to point it out to her. She had enough on her plate.

We passed another one. This one said:

STEVE – GO TO THE LIBRARY.

I gripped the sides of my seat. I touched my hat. It hit me like a punch. Someone, or something wanted us to go to the library.

I thought about the package.

I thought about my hat.

I thought about Mrs Prothero.

'I think we should go to the library,' I said.

Mum just ignored me. If anything, she drove faster.

We pulled off the Western Distributor Road and onto the roundabout to the retail park. We slid past the computer shop and the shoe shop and came to a halt at the supermarket.

I decided not to go on about the library, at least not until I'd made sure Mum was OK. She must be upset. I sprang out of the car and went off to fetch a trolley.

'What a day,' I said, as we rolled into the supermarket.

She smiled. 'Yes, Steve, it was a bit stressful.'

'First Dad's birthday, then the collapsing lady and finally – poor old Steve. But don't worry. I'm Spirit of Steve and I'm here to help.'

Mum was holding a box of Shreddies.

'What?' she asked. She had a kind of cross look on her face.

Mum is a very calm person. But sometimes she gets angry. You can tell when she's losing it because first she goes red in the face, then her eyes go fiery and then she shouts, loudly. I don't mean that in an ordinary way. I mean that in an extra-ordinary way.

She shouts – LOUDLY. It's a three-step process. Once you notice it happening, there's nothing you can do to stop it.

1. Mum started to go red. It was happening.

'Wait!' I said. 'I'm the ghost of your son, Steve. I want you to know, he doesn't blame you.'

2. Mum's eyes went fiery. That was the second step done.

I looked around, I was desperate for some way of stopping her. 'Don't go nuts. Count to ten. Try not to blame yourself,' I said, but it was too late.

3. 'STEVE!!!!!' she shouted, waving the packet of Shreddies in the air. 'I'VE HAD ENOUGH.'

Everyone in the aisle turned their heads and watched.

'You're not dead,' shouted Mum. 'You passed out in the dentist's chair. We had to take you into the front garden and wave towels in your face. You fainted. Just like Mrs Prothero.'

'You mean, I'm not Spirit of Steve?' I asked.

'Of course you're not,' said Mum. Now she was smiling. 'You're Steve. Real Steve.'

I thought about this for a minute. That made sense. I sighed with relief. 'Thanks for telling me,' I said.

She laughed. Mum doesn't stay shouty for long and I was glad to be back alive. I had a lot to live for.

I hugged her – she'd been through a lot.

Mum grabbed the trolley and we moved on to my favourite part of the supermarket: the big freezers where they keep the frozen chips. I like jumping up on the side just to get a waft of the cool air from inside.

'Crinkle-cut or straight?' asked Mum.

'Crinkle,' I said, 'we had straight last week.'

'Jaydee prefers straight.'

'She straightens her hair: she's a straight-a-holic.'

Mum pushed the freezer lid right open. There were plenty of packets of straight chips. But just one crinkle-cut packet. It was in the far left-hand corner. Mum leant but she couldn't quite reach.

'Come on, Steve,' she said, 'just have straight – they're all the same.'

Mum was clearly losing her grip. Nobody in their right mind would say crinkle-cut chips and straight chips were the same. I pushed myself up on the side of the freezer and leaned right in so that my feet tipped off the ground. I reached out as hard as I could and grabbed the last crinkle-cut chip product with the tips of my fingers.

I was off-balance on the edge of the freezer, stretching as hard as I could. My head was actually resting on the packets of straight chips. Then I saw it. In between two straight packets.

A blue dummy!

I yanked the crinkle-cut chips out as fast I could and stepped back from the freezer.

'What now, Steve?' said Mum.

I went back for another look. There it was, a little blue dummy, furred up with a layer of ice crystals. I grabbed it and pulled it out. I knew I couldn't tell Mum what I'd found.

'Nothing,' I said, shoving the dummy in my pocket.

We finished the shopping and went home. Mrs Etherington called, after her tennis match, to make me a new appointment and check that I was OK. I was OK.

I realised, as I climbed up into bed that night, what a lucky escape I'd had.

But now I had found something even more worrying.

I lay on the top bunk, still wearing my lucky library hat, listening to Kyled snoring below, staring up at the turquoise summer night sky through the skylight. I held the frozen dummy up. It wasn't icy any more. And in a way, that made it even worse.

I had known it was strange straight away.

Something to be investigated. But it had taken me this long to work out what it must mean. Still there, way down beneath those bags of straight-cut frozen chips, there must be – an *ice baby*. It may have fallen in, it may have crawled in, it may even have been placed there by some cruel childminder. It didn't matter. I knew I would have to go back to the freezer. I had to rescue the ice baby. The only thing I couldn't work out was what it all had to do with the library.

I looked up at the night sky, framed by the neat square of my skylight. A shooting star slid across the pane. I followed it with my eyes as it slit the sky in two.

The star stopped. I watched it for ages. It didn't move. I stood and pushed the window above my head open.

After all this time watching the sky something had finally happened. The star didn't move.

I stepped out onto the roof to get a closer look.

6

The Library Of Dreams

'Well, have you got it?'

'What?' said Steve, spinning on his heels, trying not to disturb the roof slates or lose his balance.

Steve searched the sky for the slow-moving star. But something strange obscured his vision; something so odd that it took his breath away. Not far from the roof, floating above the trees, he could make out a huge stone archway and it was moving towards him. The entrance was curved, like a church door and inside he could see a vast flame-lit room. Orange light spilled out through the archway and shadowy figures hurried around inside. Steve moved towards the archway. But his feet kocked the tiles and he almost slipped off the roof.

'You are Steve? This place is Oliphant Circles, near Newport in some weird place called Wales?' said the voice. The voice seemed to be outside and inside Steve's head at the same time.

Steve steadied himself and looked out into the night. He could see a figure leaning on one of the columns by the entrance. The entrance slid closer. It was almost like a spaceship, except it was made of stone and it looked like the entrance to St Esther's church.

'Wales?' whispered Steve.

'Don't tell me we've messed up the coordinates,' said the voice, 'I'm really sorry. I thought we were in a small, almost unheard of country called Wales, I thought I was talking to a small, totally unheard of boy called Steve.'

As the doorway moved closer to the roof, Steve saw more of the man. His face was wide, with a smile like a crack in a teacup. His shiny, bright, little blue eyes glinted in the firelight and his grey hair stuck out from the rim of his pork-pie hat like a crown.

'What d'you want?' asked Steve shakily.

'The dummy, dummy,' said the man, looking around. 'This isn't what I'd expected, when they said you lived in Wales I thought you'd be up on a mountain looking after a flock of sheep. This place is flat, it's got roundabouts and a KFC.'

Steve shoved his hand into his pyjama pocket. He sighed with relief as his fingers clenched the blue dummy he'd found among the chips. He held it out.

'This is a new town,' he stammered, 'it's not very new though. And Newport, which is nearby, is actually old and it doesn't…'

'Spare me the geography lesson,' said the man, taking the dummy and holding it up to his eye, like a diamond.

Steve could see through the arch now. Huge flaming torches hung from the sides of massive stone columns within. Steve took a step towards the man. A roof tile skittered down and landed on the ground with a crash.

'How do you know about the dummy?' asked
Steve, sticking his arms out, trying to keep his
balance.

Steve took another step, now the huge arched
entrance was so close he could reach it. He stuck his
foot out.

'Go on,' said the man, 'one giant leap for mankind.'

Without warning everything changed. Suddenly Steve found himself inside the building looking out at night-time over Oliphant Circles and Pendown. He could see the distant hills and the roof tiles and the open window through which he'd scrambled and the slow-moving star dragging itself across the sky.

Steve turned his back on his house. Inside the building was like a cathedral. A forest of ancient-looking circular columns rose up. Torches burned on staircases and stacks of books and scrolls of paper were piled high in corridors and on walkways. Between them, people wearing loose-fitting, hooded brown robes hurried backwards and forwards. They never spoke. They just scuttled past with their books and paper.

The man in the pork-pie hat was still there, leaning on the inside of the doorway.

Steve hesitated. He stepped back.

Suddenly Steve was back on the outside. The walls, columns and floor shrunk back and Steve was tottering on the rooftop, wobbling in the night air. Another slate slid from under his feet and crashed down to the ground. This time Steve jumped towards the entrance. The walls shot forward surrounding him in the enormous building. He was back on the inside. As his eyes grew accustomed to the orange glow of the lanterns he began to see rows of wooden booths stretching away through the corridors of columns for what looked like miles. Above them were staircases leading to infinity of smaller rooms and rickety-looking bridges between the columns.

'Stop playing games, Steve,' said the man. 'You haven't got much time. You can't stay at home with your mam forever. You've got to step out.'

Steve hesitated.

'What? Where? Why?' he stammered.

'This,' said the man, proudly, 'is the Library of Dreams. Don't ask too many questions, it'll freak you out. Where have you been by the way?'

Steve blinked at the man. He flicked the brim of Steve's hat.

'We've been trying to contact you, but you've ignored our messages. It's very irritating.'

Steve pulled his hat off.

'You sent me this?'

'Fat lot of good it did,' said the man, as he moved away from the entrance.

The man stuck the dummy in his mouth. He seemed to be tasting it. He nodded slowly.

'Yep, it's the right one,'

'Whose is it?' asked Steve.

'The Ice Baby's, I guess that's why you crossed the line.'

Steve didn't like to say that he didn't really know where he was or why. He guessed he was having some kind of dream or nightmare, but he had never had a dream before which had actually taken him out through the window and onto the roof.

'Who are you?' he asked. 'I've never heard of the Library of Dreams.'

The man smiled.

'Nobody's heard of you or Oliphant Circles but it doesn't mean you don't exist.'

Steve nodded his head, confused.

'The name's Big Mo,' said the man, extending his hand and shaking Steve's. 'Step this way, you need to get ready. It'll be very cold where you're going; you'll need weapons and some information.'

Big Mo opened the door to one of the wooden booths. Inside, behind an old, ink-stained desk, sat a young man wearing a brown-hooded robe. In front of him, resting on the desk, were a pile of sheepskins and a round stone. On the wall behind him was a map, it was all white, apart from one dot in the bottom left-hand corner. Next to the dot were the words 'Mount Gneargh'. And then, in brackets, the word 'dangerous'.

'Ah, you're in here,' said Big Mo to the man. 'Steve, this is one of our librarians. I asked him to bring as much as he could about the Ice Baby situation.'

Rather apologetically the man held out the stone. He spoke in a quiet, timid voice. His face was pale and Steve noticed that he wouldn't look him in the eye. It was almost as if he was embarrassed about something. Or ashamed.

'We're a little short of information,' stammered the librarian. 'You see, at the Library of Dreams we pride ourselves on knowing everything, or at least everything anybody ever dreamt of. When you think about it that means we know about more than everything. Things that don't exist, do exist here. In fact, everything anyone makes up exists in here. The problem is that sometimes stuff gets forgotten. That's when we have to act – if you like – we restore them.

And to do that we need help. All the librarians you've seen, we can't leave the library, we're librarians. We need volunteers like you to do our work in the real world. And there have been a lot of cutbacks.'

'Speak up, man,' shouted Big Mo.

The librarian took a big gulp of air.

'Steve, we're very pleased you picked up our distress signal.'

'The dummy?' asked Steve. 'We took a great deal of time and effort placing it in that freezer full of straight-cut chips. We have to select our agents carefully and you'd ignored all our other signs. The hat, Mrs Prothero, all of our usual methods of communication didn't work on you. Only someone with a particular kind of intelligence, curiosity and a will to win would have found the Ice Baby's Dummy.'

'You mean, there's no frozen baby?' asked Steve.

'Yes, of course there is, but not in the freezer,' said the man at the desk, still hiding his face in the shadows of his hood. 'The baby we want you to help is a little harder to reach. It's in an ice age. Well, to be more precise, it's in the end of an ice age.'

Big Mo looked at his watch, and tapped it impatiently.

'Steve, could you stop asking questions and listen. We selected you because you've got a good imagination – use it. This is the Library of Dreams where nothing is beyond belief. Picture this,' added Big Mo. 'The last ice age on earth has finished and the great ice sheets that covered the land are retreating. The temperature is rising and the glaciers covering the place the Stone Age people call Mount Gneargh are melting.'

Mo tapped the map. The librarian nodded. He picked up the sheepskins.

'Put 'em on, Steve, you must blend in AND stay warm.'

Steve wriggled into the sheepskin coat. It reached his feet. He felt like a bear.

Mo removed Steve's hat and the librarian placed a sheepskin hat on his head and handed him a pair of sheepskin boots.

When Steve was dressed Big Mo looked at him.

'Man, you'll be safe in that lot. You look like a pile of woolly washing,' he said.

Steve didn't feel safe at all. He felt extremely worried. He looked at the rock in the librarian's hands.

'What's that for?' asked Steve.

'Ah,' said the librarian.

'Speak up,' said Big Mo, 'we haven't got all day. Steve's got a mission and he's got to sort things out before that baby freezes.'

'What mission?' asked Steve. 'You can't pick on me just because I found a dummy in the chips freezer.'

'Good thinking like that, Steve, is exactly what we at the Library of Dreams like to see,' said Big Mo, patting Steve on the back of his sheepskin coat.

The librarian handed the rock to Steve.

'It's the best we could do,' he said. 'At this time, tribes had wooden and stone tools. But we're not entirely sure what they were like. Forty thousand years is a long time and much of the evidence has been destroyed. We thought at the very least we could give you this to defend yourself with.'

Steve turned the stone over in his hands.

'It's a stone,' he said, slightly unimpressed.

'A paperweight actually. I borrowed it from the

Correspondence Section. I thought it might be better than nothing.'

The librarian smiled. Steve took the paperweight. It didn't feel like much of a weapon.

'Haven't you got any guns or lasers?' he asked.

'Wrong temporal sphere, we take care never to introduce technology from the future into the past. This stone we've just given you represents quite an achievement for early humans. That paperweight is the equivalent of a surface-to-air, computer-controlled guided missile,' said the librarian proudly.

The librarian, Steve and Big Mo all looked at the grey stone in Steve's hand. It was about the size of a grapefruit.

'Not so interesting to watch though,' added the librarian.

'Right, Steve, this is what you've got to do,' said Big Mo. 'Save the Ice Baby. Use the technology if you have to.'

'You mean the rock,' said Steve.

Big Mo pushed open a wooden door at the other end of the booth. Steve gasped as snowflakes fluttered in from the frozen world beyond the threshold.

'This is what you need to know, the year is 43,567 years BC; the last Neanderthal tribes are being pushed out of Europe by human beings. The human beings don't understand that to survive they have to team up with the Neanderthal people. Instead they're just killing them. The place we're sending you to is where the very last Neanderthal baby lives, it's a big mountain. The locals who live in these parts call it "'Mount Gneargh".'

Steve blinked at Mo. He found it difficult to follow what he was saying. Everything was happening too fast. Steve scratched his eyes. He looked at Mo as if he couldn't quite believe he was real.

'Is this a dream?' he asked.

Mo ignored him. Steve was in the Library of Dreams; of course it was a dream. Steve's problem, thought Mo, was that he didn't realise how important

dreams are. That in fact what most people call 'real'
life is actually controlled by dreams – by the Library
of Dreams.

'Oh, yes,' added Mo. 'You'll be able to understand
everyone and everyone will be able to understand

you – everything will be translated. Off you go,' said Mo, shoving Steve towards the door.

'Good luck,' said the librarian sadly.

'Hang on a minute,' said Steve. 'What do I do when I get there? Why do I need to save this Ice Baby anyway?'

'Because if you don't, the humans will kill the last Neanderthal baby, and by doing that they'll destroy themselves. They don't know it – but all modern humans are made of a mixture of Neanderthal and human. That little baby has to survive.'

'What if I can't save the Ice Baby?' asked Steve.

'We're all done for,' said the librarian gloomily.

'I see,' said Steve, 'no pressure then.'

'Bye, Steve,' said Big Mo.

'You can't just push me out there,' said Steve.

'I'm afraid I can,' said Big Mo, pushing Steve to the door. Snow and ice stretched out in front of him, mountain peaks reared up ahead.

'Oh, and don't forget this.' Big Mo handed Steve the blue dummy.

Steve blinked up at Big Mo.

'Don't worry, Steve, you'll save the day. You always do.'

'Do I?' asked Steve.

'When was the last time you didn't get out of a dream alive?' said Mo with wink.

Mo shoved Steve in the back and he stumbled out into the snow. The wooden door closed behind him with a crash. Steve spun around. The door had disappeared; now it was all snow.

7

Mount Gneargh

Steve turned slowly. He shivered. A cold blast stung his face. If he'd been on a skiing holiday he'd have thought the place was perfect. Huge snow-covered mountains rose up around him. Black cliffs of rock overhung with blue ice glaciers reflected the sunlight, forcing Steve to shield his eyes. He could hear the sound of water too. Nearby he spotted a stream cascading down a snow-lined valley. And there were other sounds. He could hear droplets of water dripping down as the ice above his head melted. The snow and ice all around was glazed with a shiny film of melting water. Splinters of ice crystals floated in puffs of wind making the air sparkle and shimmer.

Steve shivered. He felt scared, the wind was icy

cold. He was lost in a wilderness so remote nobody would believe it could be real.

'Help!' he shouted.

His voice sounded soft. It was muffled by the fat snowflakes and the big white drifts.

'Mum!!!' he yelled, 'I'm having a bad dream. Wake me up. WAKE ME UP!'

A tear ran down Steve's cheek.

Nobody woke him up.

'MUUUUUUUUM!' Steve shouted as loud as he possibly could. Nobody shook him; no friendly face appeared asking him what the matter was.

Steve stamped his foot in the snow.

'Typical,' he muttered, 'she's going to leave me out here in this dream to freeze.'

Steve shoved his hands into his pockets. They were warm and big. Whoever had made his sheepskin outfit had done a good job. He felt the stone and the blue dummy. They made him feel less lonely. The stone reminded him of the library, which was warm, and the dummy reminded him of the chips freezer in the supermarket, which was home. Steve realised that the only way to get back was to save the Ice Baby. If he didn't do that he began to believe that he would be trapped on the slopes of Mount Gneargh forever.

Steve waded through the deep snow towards the stream. The snow was thin there and it was easier to walk. Steve looked around. It was a beautiful place, but a strange and lonely one. As he approached the river a word Big Mo had used came back to him.

'Neanderthals.'

Steve didn't know much about Neanderthals, but he had heard of them in school. He knew that they were the ancestors of human beings. They were supposed to have been big, strong, thick-set creatures with heavy, bony heads. Steve knew that Neanderthals were incredibly strong, very dangerous and very, very stupid. That was why they had died out.

When he reached the side of the river, Steve scanned the scene. It was clear there were no Neanderthals around. In fact there was nothing living in sight. The white slopes of the mountains rose up to melting blue glaciers peaked with jagged black outcrops of rock. The river flowed down through a valley of rocks and snow. Steve looked up at the crystal-clear blue sky. His teeth chattered, but not with cold. He was scared. At night, Steve knew that the temperature would drop, then it was only a matter of time before the weather changed, there would be snow, there would be rain, then there would be avalanches.

As if to prove a point Steve heard the rumble rolling off a distant peak. Millions of tonnes of snow

and ice lost its grip on the mountainside and crashed down. A plume of ice dust rose up into the sky like smoke.

Steve began to follow the river. The river would lead him downwards, off the mountain, to safety.

That was his theory.

Steve trudged along the side of the stream for what seemed to be ages. When he thought he couldn't trudge any more, he carried on trudging. He trudged so much that he began to kid himself that trudging was good. He told himself not to stop trudging, to

keep following the river for as long as there was light in the sky. He had to scramble down cliffs, trudge along the wide riverbed, and balance his way through deep gorges. He kept his eyes open for bears and wolves but there was nothing other than a few big birds gliding around high above his head in wide circles. Steve had a strange feeling though. He felt as if he were being watched, not by the eagles above but by something or somebody on the ground and close by. But even though he tried to catch the creature out by spinning around suddenly or looking one way and then the other really quickly, he saw only the black shapes of rocks in the snow.

There were no trees, just a few tufts of grass on the valley floor, where the snow had melted. Steve knew he had to get further down the mountain, even if that meant trudging at night. But it got harder and harder to move forward. As the darkness deepened he couldn't see the rocks he was scrambling over, he kept falling and hurting himself. The moon and stars gave him some light, but it was really difficult for Steve to keep on his feet. The silver light reflected off the snow and the water but the rocks seemed to suck it in. It was like walking in a world full of holes. Steve didn't know whether his feet would touch something or simply slip away, tripping him over.

'Ouch,' shouted Steve, clambering to his feet. His sheepskin was heavy with ice. He was red-faced and furious. His hands and feet were cold and numb.

'You stupid rock! I didn't ask to be here. I don't want to be here. Get me out of here.'

Steve's voice echoed up the mountain. Steve closed his eyes. He hoped he hadn't set off another avalanche. He began trudging once more. But now his strides were shorter. He was hardly trudging at all. He was stumbling, blind, into the gloom on the slopes of a deserted, snow-covered mountain in a country he'd never been to at a time he could only just imagine.

At night in the mountains things go dead. The

rush of the river disappears from the ears. The crunch of feet on snow or rock becomes an imperceptible rhythm. The mind shuts out the sound and the body gets on with trudging. This is when Steve heard something.

He stopped and listened. At first he thought he must be imagining the sound. But it came back and it was as faint as the sound of a baby crying in a neighbour's house. Steve peered into the silver night towards the sound. His heart pounded. He was concentrating too hard to feel worried. Perhaps this was the Ice Baby. Perhaps this was the reason why he'd been sent to this lonely, cold mountainside.

Something caught Steve's eye, a tiny movement to his left. He turned quickly. This time he saw a shape. Steve moved forward.

'OK,' he said, 'I know you're there. Come out so I can see you.'

Slowly, Steve edged towards the boulder.

'Come out,' shouted Steve, 'I know you're there.'

Steve was too tired to be scared. Before he could weigh up whether he was right or wrong he jumped behind the rock. He was fed up with not knowing things.

But there was nothing there. Steve bent down and looked at the snow. His eyes widened and his mouth opened as his hand traced the shapes in the snow. They weren't paw prints, they were footprints. Then he saw it, lying on the snow, wrapped in animal skins, blue with cold, it was a baby – an ice baby. It let out a friendly gurgle. Steve stretched out his hand. He smiled at the baby.

'Hello there,' he said, 'you must be the Ice Baby.'

Steve felt something cold slap into the side of his head. The force of the blow sent him crashing across onto the snow. As he slid on the cold silver ice Steve twisted his head and saw a figure, taller than him, wearing an animal skin like him. The figure held a stick with both its hands. It ran at Steve swinging the stick at Steve's head.

Steve's head was still swimming after the first whack. He managed to move to one side as the log came down, splatting into the ice inches from his nose. Steve pushed his hand into his pocket. He felt the dummy. That was the last thing he wanted. He threw it at the baby. He felt the librarian's paperweight. He pulled it out as the attacker took another swing at his head. When the log hit the ground Steve threw the stone with all his strength at the attacker's head. It hit. The attacker stood still for a moment, wobbled and then collapsed into the snow.

Steve clambered to his feet. He felt quite pleased

with himself as he dusted snow off his sheepskin. He walked over, picked up his lucky rock and popped it back into his pocket. Then he turned to the body in the snow. What kind of Neanderthal would it be? A hairy one? A spotty one? A crossed-eyed one with no front teeth? Steve wanted to get a glimpse of the creature he'd just destroyed with his stone. He pulled at the beast's woolly hat. What he saw made him cry out loud with surprise and shock.

It was a girl. Her black hair was matted and her skin was white as the snow. Her eyes were closed. Steve moved closer. He knelt down and put his ear next to the girl's mouth. She was still breathing. He looked around. He had no idea what to do. The girl was taller than Steve, he guessed she might have been the same age as his sisters. She looked a little like Jaydee.

Steve buried his head in his hands – his dream was becoming a nightmare. It felt far worse doing bad things to other people than having terrible things done to him.

'NO!,' shouted Steve as he stared at the girl, 'why did you do that?'

He was disgusted with himself. He felt the mountains turn their backs on him. He knew that if he could he had to help the girl. He hadn't meant her any harm.

Steve looked around desperately. It was getting very, very cold. He realised they had to get off the mountain before the frost swallowed them all in a snowdrift forever. Steve tried pulling the girl to her feet, but she was unconscious. He tried carrying the baby and dragging the girl, but the girl was too heavy. In the end Steve sat down on the ground next to the girl. He looked down at the baby in his arms. It was sucking the blue dummy. Steve remembered his mum. She hated dummies. She said they deformed babies' teeth and made them look stupid. He hoped the Ice Baby's parents didn't mind dummies. He wished the girl would get up. She'd be able to get them off the mountain. She'd know the way down.

Whack. Something hit Steve, hard. This time it knocked him out cold too.

When Steve woke up it wasn't cold or dark any more. He could smell smoke and feel the warmth of a fire and he could hear birds, nice small tweeting birds. He blinked as he sat up, rubbing his head. It hurt. It was the biggest headache he'd ever had. Even bigger than the one he had when he had to go to the doctor with suspected migraine. Slowly things came into focus. He was lying on a bed of pine needles under a tall spiky tree near a smoky fire in a forest.

Steve sat up. Two people looked at him: a very old woman, bent almost double, and the young girl. Both wore clothes made from animal skins, like his. Around their necks they had necklaces made of shells. They stood and watched as Steve sat up. They seemed to be waiting for him to do something. But Steve didn't know what to do. He stared at the old lady.

'Did you hit me?' he asked, incredulously.

The old lady grinned and nodded.

Then Steve heard a different sound, not the birds, or the spitting of the damp wood in the fire. He

heard a noise that reminded him why he was there in the first place. A baby began to cry. Steve turned and saw the baby. It was lying next to him, wrapped in skins, sucking on the dummy. It looked up at Steve and smiled. The baby seemed pleased to see Steve.

'Err – is this the Ice Baby?' asked Steve.

'Are you Steve?' asked the girl.

'Who's she?' asked Steve, pointing at the old woman.

'My gran,' said the girl.

'Can you explain what's going on?' asked Steve. 'I thought I was having a bad dream, then a nightmare, but now I'm not so sure. Does your mum do Spanish lessons?'

The girl looked at the old woman. The old woman nodded, she seemed to trust Steve.

'Steve,' said the girl, 'you're the answer to our prayers.'

Steve scratched his sore head.

'You've been sent to help us. My grandmother has prayed, I have prayed, even the little baby has prayed. 'Send us a warrior to get us out of this mess.' That is what we asked of our gods.'

'They sent you,' said the old woman. 'You must be a beginner warrior. Is this your first time?'

Steve blinked at the old lady.

'What mess?' he asked. 'What exactly is the problem?'

'This little baby is my brother,' said the girl. 'We are all that remains of our tribe,' said the girl.

Steve had a bad feeling about the news he was hearing.

'The others were killed by the humans,' said the girl.

'Hold on a minute,' said Steve, 'aren't you human?'

'Of course not,' said the girl, proudly, 'I'm a halfling.'

Steve wasn't sure what a halfling was. The girl sighed impatiently.

'A long time ago this place was shared between two tribes of people. Tall, thin humans, and short strong Neanderthals. They were friends. My mother was a human and my father was a Neanderthal,' said the girl. 'Then the food started to run out and the humans organised themselves. First they killed the Neanderthals, then the halflings, now they kill any human who helps a halfling or a Neanderthal. We're all that's left. The three of us.'

Steve looked at the old woman.

'Is she a halfling too?' asked Steve.

'Don't be ridiculous, she could have killed you when she hit you. She didn't use a stick to knock you out. She's a one-punch wonder. That's what we call her – One Punch. She's a full-on Neanderthal. The very last one.'

'Pleased to meet you, One Punch,' said Steve.

One Punch nodded and smiled.

'We came up the mountain to search for you,' said the girl. 'Our gods told us you would be there.'

'Don't tell me,' said Steve, 'do your gods speak to you when you're asleep.'

The old lady laughed.

'You see how wise he is,' she cackled. 'He's the warrior we have been promised and no mistake.'

'We thought you were trying to kill us. It was the sign you gave us that saved your life. One Punch was just about to pull your heart out so that the baby could have a nice warm drink of blood. But our gods predicted that Steve would bring peace to the starving baby,' said the girl, 'that's what you did.'

The girl pointed at the baby happily sucking its dummy. Steve shifted uneasily in his sheepskin boots.

The girl and One Punch looked at Steve.

'Well?' they said.

'Well, what?' said Steve.

'You're the warrior sent by the gods,' said the girl. 'Tell us what to do.'

Steve thought for a moment. He glanced back at the high snow-capped mountains. He remembered the icy cold and the dreadful silence of the cold dark slopes. Then he remembered his mother's Spanish class.

'We should head south,' he said. 'If we go up into the hills we'll freeze to death. The south is always warmer, that's what they say in the Spanish class.'

'Very well,' said One Punch, 'the warrior has spoken. Let it be so.'

One Punch began marching away, through the pine trees. The girl threw earth on the fire to put it out, picked up the baby and followed. Steve ran after them.

'Aren't you going to ask why?' said Steve. 'I could be wrong.'

'It's a crazy idea,' said One Punch. 'Heading south takes us straight through hostile lands held by the human tribes. But who knows, if we can get to the other side, they do say there are wide empty spaces beyond. That's if the cats don't eat us.'

'The cats?' echoed Steve.

'They're not exactly "cats",' said the girl hurrying after One Punch. 'They are more like tigers, but with great long teeth like swords. Nobody would ever try to get past them.'

'And there's the swamps,' said One Punch to the girl, 'I'd like to see how he's going to get us through that.'

Steve ran after them.

'You see,' said One Punch, 'he knows how to take risks. He looks and sounds stupid, but he's definitely got the mind of a warrior. Only a real warrior would come up with a bold plan like that.'

'Marching south to the empty lands – wow!' agreed the girl, happily. 'If he wasn't a great warrior, we'd certainly be killed by the humans.'

'Mashed to pieces,' said One Punch, then she started whistling.

The girl turned and looked back at Steve as he hurried towards them through the trees.

'That is one dangerous plan,' she said. 'You must be awfully good.'

Steve swallowed. Maybe he'd made a mistake.

'You've heard that there's a place in the south where we can be free. You know the stories about the places where the Neanderthals can live freely, far away from the horrible human beings.'

'Look,' panted Steve, 'I'm not a real warrior. I'm just a boy. I'm scared of fighting. When I see danger I go indoors. Honestly, I'm really scared. I can't help you.'

But the Neanderthal and the halfling girl ignored him and hurried away into the forest.

8

Flesheaters

One Punch, the baby, the girl and Steve walked (or in Steve's case ran) down the sloping land on the side of the mountain. The girl carried the baby in the sling on her back. Both she and her grandmother stepped silently across the ground. Their feet seemed to float over the beds of pine needles. It was Steve who blundered along, splitting twigs, slipping on needles and falling into potholes.

Every time Steve made a noise One Punch and the girl exchanged glances, as if to say that they didn't understand why Steve was so useless at keeping quiet, after all, he was supposed to be a good warrior. They didn't stop for food; they just kept going, resting every hour. The girl and One Punch seemed very nervous. They wanted to get out of the forest as quickly as possible. They kept looking over their shoulders, as if they knew they were being followed. Sometimes they'd stop and listen. Then they'd exchange glances and hurry along, even faster. The Ice Baby slept in its sling, sucking on the blue dummy happily.

'You know you shouldn't really let them have dummies all the time,' said Steve.

The girl glared at Steve.

'Steve, if the humans don't get us, the sabretooth tigers will, and if they don't get us, then we'll drown when we cross the great swamps, and if that doesn't happen there's always the lions. The journey south is impossibly dangerous. I'm not going to stop the baby from having this "dummy". It's entitled to some pleasure. Anyway, you gave it to him.'

Steve glared at the girl.

'I can't help you! I'm not a warrior. What do I know about killing tigers?' shouted Steve.

'You must be. It's been foretold!' the girl shouted back. 'Only a warrior can save us.'

'I'm not a war…'

One Punch put her finger to her lips.

'Sshshh,' she said, gazing into the green and black world of pine trunks and needles.

'Humans,' she added, sniffing the air with her nose. 'About forty or fifty, coming from that direction, maybe a mile off.'

The three travellers moved off. This time One Punch and the girl jogged and Steve ran as fast as he could to keep up. There was a fizzing sound in the air. Steve couldn't work out what it was. It was like the flapping of birds' wings, it came closer and closer, swinging and swaying as it swished past the trees and then, with a clatter, it stopped as it crashed into a tree trunk close to Steve.

'Come on,' yelled the girl, 'run for it, we're almost out of the forest. They won't follow us beyond the forest.'

A flat piece of wood clattered to the ground as it bounced off a tree. It was about the size of a cricket bat, but bent, like a coat hanger.

'Boomerangs,' muttered Steve, 'that's just great. These things are lethal.'

He turned and shouted back into the forest.

'Have you any idea how dangerous these can be?'

Suddenly the air was full of the beating sound of the boomerangs as they curved in and around their prey. One Punch managed to knock one aside just before it struck the little baby clinging on the girl's back. Steve ducked as one almost chopped his head off. It was getting harder to run fast as the boomerangs kept swinging in from all angles. Their

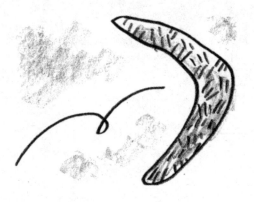

sharpened edges sliced the air like helicopter blades, filling the forest with a strange purring sound. Steve knew it was only a matter of time before they got hit.

'It's no good,' he said, 'we're going to get sliced up by Stone Age boomerang throwers. This couldn't be worse.'

'There it is,' shouted One Punch as she bounded towards the edge of the forest.

Steve looked ahead. He could see the sun's rays splashing into the forest; he could make out bright

yellow grassland ahead as another boomerang crashed in towards him. Maybe, he thought, just maybe, there would be enough time to scramble out of the forest. He ran as fast as he could. Leaping over fallen logs, shielding his head with his arms.

With screams of relief they ran free of the forest, bounding out into the open plain. Breathless, they stopped and looked back as the humans arrived at the

fringe of the pine forest. Steve watched them emerge from the dark gaps between the pine trees. Their fur skins fluttered in the breeze blowing in off the plain. The men had long straggly hair, some had plaited it into dreadlocks, they had beards, and patterns painted on their legs. They looked wild and ferocious. The biggest of them stepped forward. Steve guessed he was almost seven feet tall. He looked like one of the trees he lived in. On his head he wore a wooden crown, with pine cones and ivy leaves decorating the top.

'That's their king,' said the girl helpfully.

'King Headcase,' said One Punch and she spat on the grass. 'He's a total nutter.'

'Halflings,' shouted the king, 'you have a choice. Return to us and accept your fate, or continue into the Plain of Beasts and find yourself providing light refreshments for some of the best eaters the animal kingdom has ever produced.'

Then he laughed. Then all the tribesmen laughed.

Steve didn't laugh. He watched them, laughing out

loud at a joke that wasn't funny. He'd met people like this in school. He didn't like them.

One Punch looked at Steve; he could see from the way her eyes sparkled that she had an idea. He was glad. He didn't have any ideas.

'Challenge him,' said One Punch.

'Brilliant,' said the girl.

The baby sucked on its dummy, its brown eyes were wide open, it gurgled with pleasure.

'Sorry?' said Steve. 'Am I missing something?'

'Return to the forest and we will treat you with the respect a Halfling deserves,' yelled King Headcase. 'We will not kill you immediately, we will put you to work making boomerangs,' he urged, walking menacingly along the fringes of the forest. 'Then we will eat you. It will be a great honour for you to be consumed by the Flesheater people.'

'Flesheater people,' muttered Steve, 'nobody said they were going to eat us.'

'Challenge King Headcase to mortal combat,' said

the girl. 'When you kill him they'll be so frightened we'll be able to slip away.'

'Can't we just slip away anyway?' asked Steve.

'We have to stay near the forest, Headcase is right, we'll be cat meat before you can say, "Oh look, there they are",' said One Punch, pointing at a gathering group of sandy-skinned, sabretooth tigers meandering menacingly closer as they gathered in the long grass nearby.

Desperately, Steve glanced behind him. He saw tigers with teeth like he'd never seen before. Each tiger had a pair of massive fangs pointing

downwards from the upper jaw. They prowled around one another, occasionally glancing at Steve and his friends. Steve felt that one big tiger, with huge yellow fangs, seemed to be concentrating on him. He watched as the tiger's slobbery tongue rolled around its teeth. Steve realised there was no way of getting past the tigers. Somehow he had to deal with the flesh-eating human beings.

Steve surveyed the forest edge – Headcase and his tribe edged forwards. As well as boomerangs Steve could see wooden spears and wooden knives.

'Go on, Steve,' said the girl in an excited voice, 'we prayed for this.'

'Really?' asked Steve.

'King Headcase,' snarled One Punch, 'our warrior, Steve, who runs like a pig and stinks like a human, has come here to save us. He has something to say.'

One Punch shoved Steve forwards.

Steve stumbled towards the king, holding his woolly hat on his head with his hand.

'Errr, now listen here, King Headcase,' said Steve.

'You are not a Neanderthal,' said the king, sniffing the air, 'you have the smell of a human, like us. You are one of us.'

'Actually, I'm a warrior,' said Steve. 'And I must say I think you're being very unfair on my friends. You must leave them alone. Go away.'

One Punch looked at the girl; the girl shrugged. They weren't impressed.

The king laughed. He put his hands on his sides and he roared with laughter. His tribesmen joined in.

'One puny traitor against King Headcase and his brothers from the forest. My friend, if you don't join us now, you and the halflings will be ripped to pieces by my warriors and your bones sacrificed to the tigers.'

Something happened to Steve. As he watched Headcase and the tribe laughing at him, a new feeling came over him. He didn't quite understand why, but he stopped feeling so scared. A hot flush

filled his face. His cheeks went red. It wasn't fair that King Headcase could bully them. Why should he get away with killing off the Neanderthals? Why should he let this king person push him around? He felt angry.

'I challenge you,' growled Steve.

King Headcase and his warriors roared with more laughter.

Steve stumbled backwards. He couldn't believe what he'd just done. But he still felt angry.

'Me and you – one on one. I win, we go free – you win … errr, I guess it's steak and chips all round.'

King Headcase seemed to like the idea of being challenged, he leaped forwards. His warriors cheered. One Punch and the girl did a high five.

'Go on, Steve, hit him with the right, then the left, then use the jab. One, two, one, two.'

Steve stepped forward. Headcase met him. Steve looked up at Headcase, he was tall and muscly with a fearsome scar across his jaw. Headcase looked down at Steve, dressed like a ball of fluff, and laughed.

Crack! Headcase smashed Steve in the face with his fist sending him flying. Steve's sheepskin hat flew off and the sabretooth tigers edged a few feet closer.

Steve pulled himself to his feet. He suddenly realised what a terrible mistake he'd made. He wasn't a warrior. He wasn't even good at fighting. He was going to die. He looked desperately at the girl. She put her hands over her eyes. For a warrior sent by the gods, Steve seemed strangely bad at mortal combat.

Smash, smash. King Headcase landed two punches on Steve's midriff then he grabbed him in a bear hug and tossed him in the air. The warriors laughed as Steve landed on the floor.

Steve looked around desperately. He knew he needed to do something. But what?

Thwack. Headcase kicked Steve's head, making his nose bleed. Steve stuffed his hand in his pocket looking for a handkerchief. His hand touched the librarian's stone. He pulled it out and staggered to his feet. He'd had an idea.

Steve held the stone forwards and looked at Headcase.

'You see this?' he said. His brain was racing at a hundred miles an hour.

Headcase took a step back, his eyes shifted from side to side. He seemed worried about the stone.

The king edged backwards, his eyes fixed on the stone in Steve's hand. Steve edged forwards.

'A stone,' said Headcase, 'nobody said anything about stones. Where did you get it from, boy? That's a weapons grade military stone, if I'm not mistaken.'

'It's one of the most powerful hand stones in the world. It could take your head clean off,' said Steve.

The king took another step back. Steve advanced. He could hardly believe what he was doing.

The girl looked at One Punch, she smiled. Somehow, Steve was winning.

'Those boomerangs of yours are no match for this. Wooden stuff is yesterday's news – from now on, this is the Stone Age, and the one with the best stone wins.'

'OK,' said the king, 'let's not be too hasty. Hasty is wasty.'

'He almost took my head off with that thing,' shouted the girl.

The warriors shrunk back into the fringes of the woods.

Steve lined his shot up, he knew he had to hit the king square on the head – if he did that and Headcase dropped, the fight would be won. He put the stone in his right hand and got ready to throw.

'Man,' said King Headcase, 'you didn't think we were really going to eat you?'

'Let us go,' snarled Steve, 'that's all we want. Let us walk south along the fringes of the forest so that we don't have to face the tigers.'

'Is that all you want?' said Headcase. 'Of course, but give me the baby and the girl. Just to finish off this whole sorry episode with the Halflings. We should have exterminated the Halflings ages ago.'

'No!' said Steve, 'The Halflings have got just as much right to be here as you.'

Suddenly, rage flooded through the king's face. He glared at his warriors then he turned on Steve.

'Nobody contradicts a Headcase,' he shrieked and he rushed towards Steve.

Steve felt like running. But he knew he couldn't. He felt like hiding. But there was nowhere to hide. He felt like crying out for help. But there wasn't any. He tried to stay calm. He waited. Headcase bounded

closer. He was huge, with shoulders as broad as widescreen televisions. As he charged, screaming at the top of his

voice, Steve could see that his long beard was plaited with finger-bones. The king rushed at Steve and the warriors cheered. One Punch and the Girl shouted as loud as they could. Steve lifted his arm; he waited and waited, until it was almost too late. And then he threw the stone. It struck the king on the head, splitting his wooden crown and sending him crashing to the floor at Steve's feet.

The warriors drew back.

Steve couldn't believe his eyes. Tentatively, he approached the collapsed king. His eyes were closed, his breathing was slow and regular. He was out cold. Steve picked up the stone and tossed it from hand to hand, like a cricket ball.

'Let that be a lesson to you,' shouted Steve.

One Punch, the girl and even the baby all shouted for joy.

The sabretooth tigers slipped away into the long grass.

The tribesmen pulled their leader, groaning, and holding his head, back into the woods.

9

The Follower

They made camp on the fringe of the forest. They'd left King Headcase and his tribe of Flesheaters behind and travelled as far south as they could, tracking the boundary of the forest. As they walked Steve got the feeling that they were being watched. But every time he checked he saw only the forest to his left and the plains to his right.

It was night-time, when Steve asked the question. The Ice Baby had drunk its Neanderthal baby drink of goats' milk, crushed pine nuts and dried reindeer blood and had fallen asleep under a tree. The girl, One Punch and Steve were sitting by the fire. They were eating rabbit which they'd cooked over the flames. Above them they could see millions of stars casting a silvery glow over the plains ahead. All around they could hear the creatures of the night. Frogs croaked, bats twittered and mice scurried through the vegetation. The tigers stayed away. The firelight frightened them.

Steve poked the fire with a stick. Steve looked at the girl.

'What's your name?' asked Steve.

The girl looked at Steve.

'I haven't got one,' she said sadly. 'My people were destroyed by the humans before I was named. In our way of life you can't be named until people know what you're like.'

Steve nodded. He poked the fire, thoughtfully, with a stick.

'That seems quite sensible,' said Steve. 'I think I was a Steve before I was even born.'

The girl laughed.

'You really were very brave today,' she said.

Steve didn't feel brave. He wished he did.

'Can we give you a name?' said Steve.

'Names can only be given by the elders of our tribe,' said One Punch, who was snoozing nearby.

'But they're all dead,' said Steve. 'We can't just call her "girl" all the time.'

One Punch looked unconvinced.

'Very well,' she said, 'but remember, I'm her grandmother, it should be me that chooses the name.'

'Hey,' said the girl, 'don't I get any say about this?'

'Yes,' said Steve, 'let her choose – she could be Jaydee, or Miffany.'

'Jaydee?' said the girl, flicking her hair, 'what a pretty name.'

'The name you shall be called,' said One Punch, looking serious and solemn, 'is Rock Face, because you have been struck on the head by Steve's incredible stone. Let it be known to all that from this point on you shall be known as Rock Face.'

'No way,' said the girl, 'I want to be Jaydee.'

'No you don't,' said Steve.

'Why can't I be Jaydee?' said the girl.

As they argued deep into the night, a lone human watched them from the safety of a branch high up in a tree.

10

The Cat

The journey from Headcase's pine forest to the Misty Swamps should have been straightforward. They'd crossed the tiny gap between the forest and the swamp quite easily. When they arrived at the first green shoots of the swampland, they thought they'd escaped unnoticed. It was Steve who spotted the sabretooth tiger. It was lying on the grassland next to the swamp. It was thin and dehydrated.

One Punch came and took a look.

'It's too skinny to eat,' she said. She looked up at the sky. The same birds that Steve had noticed in the mountains were circling above.

'The vultures will pick at it for a few days.'

Steve looked sadly at the huge cat. Its eyes blinked slowly. He could hear its breathing was fitful.

'Groucho,' he muttered.

'I'll break its neck,' said One Punch, kindly.

Steve looked shocked.

'It's for the best,' said the girl. 'We must never allow animals to suffer – this is our way.'

One Punch took the big cat's neck in her arm.

The cat gulped, as if it knew that it was best to be killed.

'Wait,' shouted Steve.

He'd taken a turn carrying the baby; he felt it wriggle around in the sling on his back to get a closer look.

'I can see what's wrong with the tiger,' he said.

The Ice Baby laughed and gurgled with pleasure.

'Oh yeah,' said One Punch, 'some kind of tiger expert are you now?'

'It's obvious,' said Steve, 'look at its teeth.'

The girl and One Punch pulled the tiger's mouth open. One giant sabre tooth hung down like an ivory scimitar, the other was broken and yellow.

'That tiger's got a cracked sabre tooth, possibly with an impaction in the upper jaw – there's an infection and a good case to be made for fitting a crown or possibly even extraction.'

The girl and One Punch looked at Steve.

'How come you know such a lot about teeth?' they chorused.

'Oh, I read up on things, and I spend a lot of time in the dentist,' said Steve.

'So what do we do?' asked the girl.

'Pull the tooth out,' said Steve calmly.

One Punch approached the tiger's mouth. The tiger didn't move. It just lay there, its sad eyes staring out across the grassland. One Punch stuck out her hand; very gently she held the broken tooth between her thumb and her finger. The tiger winced. But it didn't move. Slowly One Punch took a hold of the tooth. Then with a sudden movement she pulled at the tooth with all her Neanderthal strength.

The tiger let out a yelp. One Punch fell over backwards. And the tooth stayed where it was. Steve stood up. He shoved his hand into his pocket and pulled out the stone. He tossed it from hand to hand as he thought.

'What tool could we use,' he said, 'to knock this poor tiger's fang out?'

'Use the stone!' said the girl. 'Quickly, we haven't got all day.'

Steve looked at the stone, then the animal. It closed its eyes and rested its head on the grass. If he didn't act quickly it wouldn't survive much longer. Steve walked up to the tiger. It was huge. Maybe twice as big as he was.

'You're not going to thank me for this right now,' said Steve, bending down and patting the tiger's head. He couldn't help noticing how soft and velvety its fur was. The animal opened its eyes, it almost seemed to be asking Steve for help. Steve took the stone in his right hand, lined up the tooth and, with pinpoint accuracy, knocked out the remains of the bad tooth with one blow.

The tiger flopped back on the grass.

'Run,' shouted One Punch, 'we've got to get away before it wakes up.'

'Can't we stay to make sure it's OK?' asked Steve.

'It'll be hungry,' said One Punch, 'you don't want to be around then. That thing hasn't eaten for weeks.'

Before disappearing into the dense green vegetation of the swamp Steve turned and looked back. He'd come a long way.

In the distance he could see the mountains covered with white snow, with those black rocks punching through like frostbitten fingers. He saw the slopes of open rock he'd clambered down, the pine forest where Headcase and the warriors lived, the plains with the ravenous tigers. He remembered how lonely he felt when he first stepped out onto the snow. He smiled as he thought about Big Mo, shoving him in the back and onto the ice. He could still hear his voice, echoing through his imagination: 'When was the last time you didn't get out of a dream alive?'

Something caught Steve's eye. For some time he had had the distinct impression that something or even someone was following them.

One Punch joined Steve. It was her turn to carry the baby. Steve swung the baby round and looked into its face. It slurped on the blue dummy. Steve rubbed the baby's cheek with his finger, he tickled its chin. The Ice Baby laughed, almost letting go of the dummy. Steve laughed, the Ice Baby was the best behaved baby he'd ever come across. Not like Kyled. He'd shared a room with Kyled for five years. As far as Steve could remember, Kyled had cried and jumped and snarled his way through every day.

'How will we know when we arrive at the safe place?' asked Steve, as One Punch took the baby.

'We dunno,' said the girl, 'you're the warrior, you're the one who's delivering us. You tell us.'

'How am I supposed to know?' asked Steve. 'I'm not really a warrior. I'm Steve. I live on a weird round road called Oliphant Circles and I play spot on in the back lane.'

'Oh, don't give me that,' said One Punch, 'of course you know. This swampy place,' she said, waving at the thick green vegetation ahead, the watery ground slithering with strange beetles and bugs and the air thick with flies: 'is this a safe place?'

'No, of course it isn't,' said Steve.

'Correct, it's a very dangerous place,' said One Punch triumphantly, 'you see, you do know what you're talking about.'

11

The Misty Swamps

Steve, One Punch, the girl and the Ice Baby entered the swamp. By the time they reached the water's edge, a mist had descended. It was almost impossible to tell where you had been, or where you were going.

'Lead us through the swamp, Steve,' said the girl. 'I know you can do it.'

Steve paced along the side of the swamp. He didn't see how he could go on. The watery wetland went on for miles.

'If Steve misses the path,' said One Punch, 'we'll drown, there's quicksand around here, it sucks you down; you'll never get out alive. The Ice Baby will never grow up to be a big Neanderthal, and you won't be a Halfling any more. Our whole species will have come to nothing: we'll just be a baby sucking a horrible blue dummy and girl with no name lost in a terrible lonely swamp.'

They fell silent. Steve picked his way forwards, testing the firmness of the ground with his feet. Then he fetched himself a stick from the bank. He used the stick to test the ground and edged further out into the swamp. He took the girl's hand. She took One Punch's hand. The baby lay strapped to One Punch's back, sucking on the blue dummy.

Inch by inch Steve moved forward. Soon they could neither see where they were going nor where they had been.

'Please can I be Jaydee,' said the girl, as they crept into the swamp.

'It's confusing,' said Steve, 'there can't be two Jaydees; you must be someone else.'

'Rock Face is a really nice name,' muttered One

Punch, 'I wish I'd been called Rock Face. One Punch sounds really unromantic.'

Steve stopped. The mist billowed around them. They stared into it. It was like peering into a pillowcase. It was strangely silent out in the swamp. The water beneath them was still. The air was dank and heavy. Nothing moved, nothing breathed.

'Errr,' said Steve.

'If he says he's lost I'll kill him,' muttered One Punch.

'I don't know which way to go,' said Steve.

They were completely disorientated, surrounded by quicksand and encased in heavy mist that seemed to push them downwards into the water.

'Can we just go back?' said the girl.

'I can't tell where "back" is.'

'And if you can't do that, you don't know where forward is,' added One Punch, helpfully.

'My mum's got a word for you,' hissed Steve, '"backseat driver". She says that to me all the time when I tell her to slow down.'

'Nobody's telling you to slow down, boy,' barked One Punch. 'Get going, that's what we're saying. Get going and let's get out of here.'

Steve bent down and felt the mud with his hands. If he didn't know better he would say that the water lapping around his sheepskin boots was getting deeper.

'Do they have tides around here?' he asked.

'When the ice melts on the mountains, the waters get deeper,' said the girl.

Steve's boots were soaking, the swamp was filling fast.

'Why didn't you tell me this would happen before we set off?'

'Are you saying I'm stupid?' asked One Punch.

'I just think it would have been good to have mentioned that the swamp was flooding. We're not going to die in the quicksand. We're going to drown in the meltwater from the glaciers.'

'What's that?' shouted the girl.

Everybody followed the direction she was pointing in. Steve could just about make out an object moving slowly into view. It was a very big grey-looking shape and it slid towards them like a long mean crocodile.

'A crock,' screamed One Punch, 'typical.'

Another thing she forgot to mention, thought Steve as he watched the shape. It didn't look like a crocodile to him. More like a piece of wood. He reached out, he could almost touch it. The water was deep now, above his knees. As his huge sheepskin coat soaked up the water, it pulled Steve down.

Without saying anything to the others Steve knew what to do. He let go of the girl's hand and waded off towards the shape. Even now, surrounded by water, blinded by the mist, weighed down by his sheepskin, he still felt that someone was watching him. He pushed himself forward and grabbed the floating log. He wasn't disappointed, it wasn't a log; it was a wooden canoe, fitted out with paddles and wooden storage boxes. In the front was a pile of animal skins. Steve guessed it must have come adrift upstream as the water levels rose.

'Steve,' shouted the girl, 'where are you? Come back.'

'He's gone,' said One Punch. 'They all do that, this one's just chosen a really bad moment to do a runner.'

With great difficulty Steve hauled himself into the canoe. He took the paddle and shouted.

'It's OK, I've found a boat, make a noise and I'll find you.'

'What kind of noise,' shouted the girl.

'I dunno,' said Steve, 'any kind of noise – sing.'

'What do you want us to sing?' said One Punch.

Steve paddled the canoe around, he wasn't far away but he couldn't quite pinpoint the source of their voices.

'Just sing,' he yelled. 'Don't you have a Neanderthal song, something that makes you feel really good?'

One Punch and the girl did know a song. It was the oddest thing that Steve had ever heard. One Punch and the girl sang slowly in sad, low voices. Steve could make out some of the words over the sound of the splashing paddle.

'Neanderthals don't rap, we don't do hip hop,
We hardly ever sing.
It's not that we don't like rap, and we don't like hip hop,
We just don't like to sing.'

Then they laughed. Then they sang it again, and again, and again.

As they sang, Steve was able to swing his canoe around and paddle back towards them. They kept singing when they saw his canoe. They continued as they scrambled into the canoe. They carried on singing as they paddled as fast as they could

downstream. And when they burst out from the swamp into the afternoon sunshine on the opposite bank they sang even louder. It was such a relief to be free from the miserable weight of the Misty Swamp.

Finally, they stopped singing.

'One thing I've learned about you Neanderthals,' said Steve, as they floated downstream.

'What?' asked One Punch.

'You need better songs,' said Steve.

12

Slasher

Steve lay back on the skins piled at the front of the boat, the Ice Baby nestled in next to him, with the blue dummy firmly stuffed in his mouth. Steve popped his finger in the Ice Baby's hand. He felt the little fingers wrap around his.

'You know,' he whispered, 'you're not an Ice Baby any more – you're a nice baby.'

The girl sat at the back of the canoe, guiding it with her paddle as it slipped along the surface of the river. One Punch sat in the middle of the boat issuing instructions.

'Left hand down, don't get too close to the bank,' she said.

Steve stretched out. He could feel his toes wiggling

deep in his sheepskin boots. He felt safe, happy and, for the first time, he didn't feel worried. He'd lost that nagging feeling that he was being followed. Whoever it was that had been tracking them couldn't keep up with the canoe. The mountains were far in the distance. Now they were floating down a beautiful lazy river through warm lush countryside.

He watched One Punch. She never rested, she kept going, she was strong and she meant what she said. He liked her.

He didn't notice the sabretooth tigers padding silently along both banks of the river. All Steve saw was smooth blue water, tree-lined riverbanks and rolling hills.

'This is fantastic,' said Steve, adjusting one of the skins he was leaning on.

'Don't get too comfortable,' laughed One Punch. 'We're about to pull over.'

Steve couldn't get comfortable. He yanked at one of the skins, trying to make a pillow. He guessed there would be time for a little doze in the afternoon sunlight.

But the pillow moved. Or the animal skin moved. Steve pulled it again, thinking that maybe the rocking of the canoe was shifting them around. But the skin seemed not to want to move now. Steve turned and started pulling at all the skins in the front of the boat. He threw them out of the way. Some landed in the canoe, others sploshed into the river water.

'Keep still, Steve,' shouted the girl. 'You'll tip us over.'

But Steve wasn't keeping still. Underneath the animal skins he'd found something extraordinary.

'Get back,' shouted Steve, leaping towards One Punch in the middle of the canoe.

One Punch fell forward; the girl almost dropped her paddle. Cowering behind Steve in the front of the canoe, half hidden by the animal skins, was a boy. He covered his face with his hands.

'Don't kill me,' he cried.

One Punch and Steve exchanged glances. The girl pulled the canoe out of the main flow of the river.

'Who are you?' asked Steve.

The boy shrank back.

'Have you been following us?' he demanded.

'I hid in the canoe. I wasn't expecting it to float off. I've run away.'

'Great,' snarled Steve, 'that's all we need.'

The boy sat up.

'Promise you won't kill me with your stone,' whispered the boy.

The girl eyed the boy suspiciously.

'How do you know about Steve's stone?' she asked.

'I knew it,' said Steve, 'he's been on our tail ever since we met Headcase and the Flesheaters.'

The girl approached the boy. She sniffed him. She looked at the tattoos on his arms and legs. She ran her fingers through his hair.

'I've got bad news,' she said. 'This kid is a Flesheater.'

'Don't kill me,' said the boy. 'I ran away because I hate being a Flesheater. For a start, I don't like the taste, and for seconds, I can't stand my dad.'

'My dad's in Khazakstan,' said Steve. 'I don't go running off all the time.'

'Your dad isn't King Headcase,' said the boy.

Steve sat down on the floor of the canoe. Now he buried his head in his hands.

'I thought you were so brave, standing up to him,' said the boy. 'He's such a bully. I wish I could have done it.'

Steve took a peep at the boy through his fingers.

'Do you know a kid called Toby?' he asked.

The boy looked blank.

'Tobes?' added Steve.

The boy looked even blanker.

'Take me with you,' he said. 'Take me wherever you're going. I want to get as far away from my horrible tribe as I possibly can.'

'We can't exactly send you home, can we?' said the girl, paddling the canoe towards a small beach on the riverbank.

'You can't come with us,' said One Punch. 'I'm a Neanderthal. You wouldn't want to spend the rest of your life hanging around with Neanderthals.'

'Why not?' said the boy. He looked at the Ice Baby, lying next to him. The baby watched him then smiled.

'I can help,' he said, tickling the baby under its chin. It gurgled with pleasure.

Steve hopped out of the canoe, he and the girl pulled it up onto the beach.

'I think he's kind of cute,' she said.

Steve sighed and shook his head in disbelief. The boy passed the baby to Steve. Then he jumped out of the canoe, splashing in the water.

'What's your name?' asked Steve.

'Slasher,' said the boy, quietly, 'Slasher Headcase.'

'Wow,' said the girl, 'cool name.'

Steve felt irritated, he didn't like the way the girl seemed happy with the presence of a complete stranger from an enemy tribe. But he knew that if Slasher hadn't followed them, hidden in the canoe and got washed into the swamp they would have all drowned in the mist. They'd never have made it.

'Come on,' said Steve, 'we haven't got much time left.'

Before they scrambled up the riverbank and onto the plain, Steve took Slasher aside.

'Are you scared of sabretooth tigers?' he asked.

'Petrified,' said Slasher unhappily.

'Stick with me,' said Steve.

He turned to One Punch.

'This is it,' he said, 'we're almost home.'

The old Neanderthal smiled.

'You know,' she said, 'when I first punched you in the face I thought you were going to be the most useless warrior I'd ever come across. It turns out you're not a bad warrior after all.'

'Follow me,' said Steve.

He walked away from the river and out into the plain. He knew the sabretooth tigers would be watching them.

The sun slipped down in the sky glowing like a huge orange, throwing red light across the yellow grass all around.

'What are we doing, Steve?' asked the girl, 'this place is full of tigers. They'll scoff us before sunset.'

'Just walk,' said Steve, leading the way, 'I think we'll be OK.'

They trudged out into the grassland leaving the river behind them.

Steve led the way, One Punch followed, carrying the Ice Baby on her back. The girl and Slasher hurried along at the rear chatting.

'What's your name?' asked Slasher.

'Jaydee,' said the girl.

'Wow,' said Slasher, 'cool name.'

From the top of a low hill, hidden by the long

grass, the sabretooth tigers stared at Steve, One Punch, Slasher, Jaydee and the baby. One tiger, with just one sabre tooth and a hole where the rotten one used to be, smiled, if it is possible for a sabretooth tiger to smile. The strangers who saved his life would be allowed to go free.

The baby was safe.

The tigers never came.

13

Paperwork

'Have you got the dummy?' The librarian looked up at Steve from behind his wide wooden desk.

Steve shook his head. He pointed at the rock, which he'd plonked down near the librarian's notebook next to his old sheepskin clothes.

'I've checked that off the list. According to our records we provided you with a sheepskin suit, a paperweight and a blue dummy which was positioned in a freezer full of chips in a supermarket in Pendown,' said the librarian, adding: 'we're a hat and a dummy down.'

Big Mo watched from the side, his brow furrowed.

'For goodness sake, Welshy,' he said, handing back the library cap, 'you lost the woolly hat too?'

'Actually, it was smashed off my head by a lunatic who wanted to kill me,' said Steve adjusting his pyjamas, 'and the name's Steve,' he added, 'not Welshy.'

'He didn't kill you though, did he? You should have collected the hat up and brought it back to us nicely. Next time, Steve, you'll have to be more careful,' said Big Mo.

'I just saved the last Neanderthal,' said Steve. 'We're all related to the last Neanderthal and I just saved the last Neanderthal.'

'Going on about your achievements isn't going to get that hat back,' said Big Mo.

He turned to the librarian.

'Make a note – lost in transit – we'll send someone back for it later.'

Big Mo held the door to the wooden booth open and led Steve back into the Library of Dreams. They walked back to the great arch. Steve looked out. He could see the little town of Pendown spread out beneath him. He could make out the roundabouts and dual carriageways with their bright orange lights, and the distant dark hills. He could see his street and the sloping roof of his house. The window over his bed was half open.

'Off you go,' said Big Mo.

'Wait,' said Steve, 'can I come back?'

'That depends,' said Big Mo. 'We'll have a few reports to write. We'll need to account for the lost gear. But if something comes up, you'll be the first to know.'

Mo cast his eye over the town. The first hints of blue dawn were seeping into the black night sky. Mo shoved Steve in the back and he tumbled out onto the roof. The tiles rattled as he scrabbled for his balance.

'Laters,' said Mo, as the doorway to the Library fell backwards and disappeared in the night sky.

'Wait,' cried Steve, 'what happened to the girl and One Punch? What about Slasher?'

'They're doing fine,' called Mo, as he adjusted his pork-pie hat. 'They still dream about you.'

Postscript

When Steve came down to breakfast on 30th July he felt different.

'Hi, Mum,' he said as he filled Groucho's dish.

He sat down at the kitchen table. He sprinkled some cereal into his bowl.

'Is everything all right?' asked Mum.

'Fine,' said Steve, as he began to eat his breakfast.

'No dangers? No missile attacks? No sun spots? No alien invasions?'

'Nope,' said Steve.

'No epidemics, no tidal waves, no mutant rodents crawling through the sewers?'

'Negative,' said Steve. He'd almost finished his cereal. He could see Kyled happily bouncing up and down on his trampoline through the window.

'No molten lava pouring up through a fissure in the earth's crust just in the middle of Pendown?' asked his mum.

Steve finished his cereal and went to the back door. He pulled his trainers on.

'I'm just going out the back,' said Steve. 'Maybe I'll see if Toby's around. There's something I want to tell him.'

'One thing,' said Mum, as Steve pushed the back door open. 'I know yesterday was a bit ... traumatic, but you really do need to go to the dentist.'

'Book me in for this afternoon, and please say sorry to Mrs Etherington, it won't happen again,' said Steve, with a confident tone in his voice.

'I'll be back for lunch at about thirteen hundred hours,' he added.

As Steve picked up his football and began to stride off down the garden Mum came to the back door. She'd noticed something strange. Steve seemed normal … almost too normal. A look of concern flashed across her face.

'Steve,' she shouted. 'Is everything alright? You don't think you're dead again do you?'

'No way,' yelled Steve, then he pointed at the sky. 'I was being ridiculous. It was a terrible mistake.'

Mum nodded slowly. There was something wrong with Steve.

'There's an invisible library up there. I could be called away on another mission at any moment. I've got to explain to Toby what to do if I get stuck up there.'

Steve pointed at the sky above the roof. Mum stepped out and looked up. There was nothing there – just sky. She sighed with relief. Steve was back to normal.

Also in the Dragonfly series from *Firefly*

Dragonfly books are funny, scary,
fantastical and exciting.

Come to our website for games,
puzzles and competitions.

www.firefly.co.uk/dragonfly

Coming soon: *Pete and the Five-A-Side Vampires* by
Malachy Doyle, *Dottie Blanket and the Hilltop* by
Wendy Meddour and *Arthur and Me* by Sarah Todd
Taylor.